HOUND TOWN CHRONICLES

SUNNY ON ALERT!

A Seizure-Alert Dog Story

by Spencer Brinker

illustrated by Robin Lawrie

BEARPORT
PUBLISHING

New York, New York

Credits

Cover photo, © adogslifephoto/Fotolia.

Publisher: Kenn Goin
Editor: Jessica Rudolph
Creative Director: Spencer Brinker

Library of Congress Cataloging-in-Publication Data

Names: Brinker, Spencer, author.
Title: Sunny on Alert! A Seizure-Alert Dog Story / by Spencer Brinker.
Description: New York, New York : Bearport Publishing, [2017] l Series: Hound
    Town Chronicles l Summary: The students in Mastiff Middle School's
    sixth-grade class, meet Sunny, a working dog that helps detect siezures in
    classmate Max who has epilepsy.
Identifiers: LCCN 2016042375 (print) l LCCN 2016053538 (ebook) l ISBN
    9781684020157 (library) l ISBN 9781684020669 (Ebook)
Subjects: l CYAC: Working dogs—Fiction. l Dogs—Fiction. l
    Epilepsy—Fiction. l Middle schools—Fiction. l Schools—Fiction.
Classification: LCC PZ7.1.B7574 Su 2017 (print) l LCC PZ7.1.B7574 (ebook) l
    DDC [E]—dc23
LC record available at https://lccn.loc.gov/2016042375

For more information, write to Bearport Publishing Company, Inc.,
45 West 21st Street, Suite 3B, New York, New York 10010. Printed
in the United States of America.

10 9 8 7 6 5 4 3 2 1

CONTENTS

WELCOME TO HOUND TOWN

A Doggone Nice Place to Live!

Population:
25,000 people
20,000 dogs

CHAPTER 1

A Classroom Surprise

"Hey Raj, can you believe it?" said Allison as she approached the street corner where her best friend was waiting for her. The two sixth graders walked to Mastiff Middle School together every morning.

"Believe what?" asked Raj. He stuffed the copy of *Science Dogs*, a book he had been reading, into his backpack.

"Mr. Calhoun's making me work with Max on the **ancient** Egypt research project," said Allison. "You know, that strange kid who almost never came to school last year, and who had to wear a helmet during recess and gym class? He's supposed to finally show up today."

"Oh, yeah," said Raj. "But it's already October—where's he been? And. . . ." He paused. "What's wrong with him anyway?"

Allison unzipped her backpack and took out a stack of Golden Sunrise crackers wrapped in crinkled wax paper. She handed a cracker to Raj. "I don't know where he's been. It has something to do with **epilepsy.**" Then she added, "That's what he has."

"Oh, right," said Raj, reaching for another cracker as they walked. "Um, what is that, exactly?"

"Epilepsy? I don't know . . . *exactly*," said Allison. "But I think something is wrong with his brain."

Raj and Allison turned the corner and walked down Woofington Street. They stopped for a few minutes in front of Mrs. Baxter's house to pet her terrier, Gizmo. The dog waited on the lawn for them every morning.

After a few more blocks, Allison and Raj arrived at school. They followed the flow of students through the front doors and down the hallway. Then they walked into their classroom and took their seats. Allison scanned the room. "I don't see him," she whispered to Raj. "Maybe he's not coming today."

The bell rang, and Mr. Calhoun closed the class door. "Good morning, everyone," he said. "As you know, we're starting our research projects on ancient Egypt. With your partner, you'll begin brainstorming topics."

Tap, tap, tap. There was a soft knock at the door, and Mr. Calhoun stopped speaking. He walked over and opened the door as Allison and Raj glanced at each other.

Ms. Sante, the school nurse, leaned in through the doorway, smiled, and said, "Hi!" Her arm was draped over the shoulder of a thin boy with brown hair. His head was bent down. As she walked him into the class, the students could see that the boy was leading a beautiful golden retriever on a leash. The dog, who was wearing a red vest, wagged its tail and looked happily around the room.

CHAPTER 2

Sunny

"Welcome!" Mr. Calhoun said as he led Ms. Sante, Max, and the dog to the front of the classroom. "Class, many of you know Max Phillips, who's joining our class today. However, we also have another newcomer. Max, would you like to introduce your friend?" Mr. Calhoun motioned toward the dog, who was sitting calmly next to Max.

Max looked quickly up at Mr. Calhoun, then at Ms. Sante, and then back at the floor. "His name is Sunshine," Max said in a quiet voice. "Sunny for short." When he heard his name, Sunny looked up at Max. His tail began to wag back and forth on the floor.

The excited students began to whisper to each other. Raj leaned over to Allison and whispered, "Why is his dog allowed in school?" Allison shrugged as she noticed Max shifting his feet nervously.

"Can we pet him?" asked Tony, a boy who was missing a front tooth.

"No, you can't!" Max raised his voice at Tony. Several students seemed surprised and confused by Max's response. Max dropped his head again. He put his hand on Sunny's head, turned to Ms. Sante, and said more quietly, "They said no one should pet him."

"Max, let's go find you a seat," said Mr. Calhoun. The teacher led Max and Sunny to an empty desk as the other students watched.

Max sat down, and the dog immediately lay on the floor beside him, looking perfectly relaxed.

Mr. Calhoun returned to the front of the class and said, "Ms. Sante, would you mind explaining to the class why Sunny is here with Max?" Everyone stared and waited.

"I'd be happy to explain," said Ms. Sante. "Well, some of you might know that Max has epilepsy. It's a condition that causes temporary problems in brain activity."

Several students turned toward Max, who was staring down at Sunny. Kara, a girl with braids sitting next to Max, shifted her desk away a few inches. Allison and Raj looked at each other. Allison mouthed the words, "I told you."

"Now, epilepsy isn't **contagious**. And it has nothing to do with a person's intelligence," Ms. Sante continued. "But someone with epilepsy does sometimes have **seizures**. Does anyone know what a seizure is?"

Allison slowly raised her hand.

Ms. Sante pointed to her. "Yes?"

Allison hesitated and said, "A seizure is when your body shakes and you don't know what's happening around you. My grandma had a seizure because of **diabetes**." Max lifted his head toward Allison.

"Yes, that's right," said Ms. Sante. "Some seizures can make a person's body shake, and the person may become **unconscious**. Other seizures can make a person stare straight ahead and not move at all. Seizures can last a few seconds or several minutes. There are many different kinds of seizures, and each person with epilepsy is different. . . . So, why do you think Sunny the dog has come here with Max?"

The students looked at Sunny, and the dog looked back at the students, his tongue hanging out.

No one raised his or her hand, so Ms. Sante said, "Max? Would you like to explain Sunny's important job?"

Max nodded. He said in a clear voice, "Sunny is a working dog. It's written on his vest. His job is to tell me or my parents when I'm about to have a seizure, so I can stay safe." Max looked around to see the students' reactions. "So I don't fall and hurt myself. That's why you're not supposed to pet him—it **distracts** him from his work."

The room was quiet, then Kara asked, "But how does he know?"

"They think dogs use their great sense of smell to **detect** changes in people's bodies," answered Max. "Also, they're good at watching people. But they still have to be trained." Max reached down to scratch Sunny's head.

"Thank you, Max," said Mr. Calhoun. "And thank you, Ms. Sante. We'll have all year to get to know our new classmates." Ms. Sante said good-bye to the class and gave a quick wink to Max as she left the room.

"Now, on to ancient Egypt," said Mr. Calhoun. "Find your partners and spend fifteen minutes brainstorming topics. Max, you'll be working with Allison."

Students began moving around the classroom. Allison grabbed a

notebook and walked over to Max and Sunny. "Hey," she said as she sat down. Sunny looked up at Allison, raised his ears, and turned his head sideways. Allison smiled.

"Hi," said Max. "He sometimes does that sideways thing with his head. He probably likes you."

"I like him, too," said Allison as she shifted in her chair. "Um . . . should we try to think of a topic?"

"Yeah, sure," said Max. "Ancient Egypt is pretty cool."

CHAPTER 3

A Perfect Match

Allison and Max finally chose the discovery of King Tut's **tomb** for their research topic. Allison had been fascinated by the story of King Tut ever since her aunt Sophie had taken her to a museum exhibition on ancient Egypt last spring. To her surprise, Max had seen the same show.

On their walk home after school, Allison said to Raj, "Max seems okay. And at least we both like King Tut. Sunny gets to hang out with us, too."

"Yeah, that's cool!" said Raj. "The dog, I mean, not Tut. *Our* topic is the Egyptian mummy animals—a way better topic I think."

Allison smiled and nudged her shoulder into Raj, who laughed as he almost fell into Mrs. Baxter's garden.

A week later, Mr. Calhoun took the class to the school library to research their projects. Allison and Max were sitting at a computer desk while Sunny lay on the floor between them.

Reading from her computer screen, Allison said to Max, "It says here that Tutankhamen, or King Tut, became the ruler of Egypt when he was only nine years old!"

Raj, who had been listening from a nearby table, leaned over and said, "But how did he measure up? Get it? *Ruler . . . measure up*?" Allison rolled her eyes and looked at Max, who was smiling.

Max turned and read from his own computer. "Tut died when he was 19 years old. . . . Geez, that's scary," he said as he reached down to touch Sunny's silky fur.

Allison watched Max pet Sunny. "How did you get Sunny?" she asked. "I mean, did you get to pick him out?" Sunny's ears popped up. The dog turned around and looked up at Allison, then over to Max. He seemed to know they were talking about him.

"I didn't get to pick him. They matched us up—the people at Paws For All," said Max. "It's over in Springfield. I had to stay there for a month so Sunny and I could train together. That's why I started school so late."

Max explained that Paws For All was an organization that matched **service dogs** with kids who need help. Some kids have epilepsy and need dogs to help detect seizures. Other dogs are trained to help kids with **autism**, hearing problems, or difficulties walking.

"I was nervous at first," said Max. "But everyone was so nice, and it wasn't hard. I spent lots of time with Sunny. I had to learn different commands, so they could see if Sunny listened to me. We also did easy stuff—just watching television, walking, and hanging out together." Max paused, and then said, "And they also watched to see if Sunny could tell when my seizures would come."

Allison asked, "Could he tell?"

"Yeah," said Max. "He was really good at it. So now he can let me know when a seizure is about to happen, and I can get to a safe place. And I don't have to wear that stupid helmet anymore."

"Sunny already had three years of the training before I met him," Max continued. "But they still needed to see if we were a good match. I knew right away we were perfect together." Max bent over and gave Sunny a hug. "Right, Sunny-boy?" Sunny looked up at him. "You look hungry, pal. Don't worry. It's almost lunchtime."

Allison reached into her backpack and pulled out two Golden Sunrise crackers. She showed the crackers to Max. "Would he want one of these?" she whispered. Sunny's eyes opened wide, and his tail wagged.

Max glanced around to make sure nobody was watching. "Well, I'm not supposed to," he whispered back. "But . . . I think he'd love one. Thanks!"

Max took one of the crackers and lowered it below the table. Sunny snapped up the cracker and made a gulping noise. Several crumbs flew out of his mouth. Allison and Max both giggled.

Then Max said, "You can give the other cracker to him." Allison smiled. She lowered the cracker, and it too was quickly gobbled up, with even more crumbs flying this time. Allison laughed out loud.

"Quiet down over there," said a firm voice. It was Mr. Calhoun, who was looking at Allison.

"I guess we should get back to work," said Max.

"Yeah," said Allison. "I guess so." They both turned to their computers.

Then Allison felt something brush against her leg. She looked down. Sunny was standing between them, looking **intently** up at Max and pawing at his leg. Allison saw Max's worried face. She said, "Oh no, does this mean . . . ?"

CLANG! CLANG! Allison wasn't able to finish her sentence. A loud fire alarm suddenly rang, and both students jumped.

CHAPTER 4

Seizure!

"Okay, everyone!" The loud voice was Mr. Calhoun's. "Walk quietly over here." Students began getting up from their tables and whispering excitedly. "Line up at the door. We'll be exiting the school as quickly as possible."

Raj approached the table where Allison and Max were still sitting. "I'm sure it's just a dumb fire drill," he said as students headed toward the door.

Max stood up and said to Allison in a worried voice, "What am I going to do? I'm supposed to go straight to Ms. Sante's office. It might happen in a few minutes!"

"What might happen?" asked Raj.

Allison pointed to the dog, who was still pawing at Max's leg. "It's Sunny!" she said. "He let Max know that . . . um, there might be a seizure!"

Max held Sunny's leash with both hands. As they headed to the library door, Raj said, "Well, let's go straight to Ms. Sante's office then. We just need to head around the corner when Mr. Calhoun isn't looking."

"I don't know," said Allison. "Maybe Ms. Sante is already outside, and we should go outside too?" she said.

The alarm was still sounding loudly. Allison looked over at Max and saw tears welling up in his eyes. Max said in a frightened voice, "But I don't want to have a seizure in front of the whole school."

Allison made a quick decision. "All right," she said. "Raj, stand near the door and make sure Mr. Calhoun doesn't spot us, then follow us when the coast is clear."

Raj walked up next to the library door and stopped, glancing around him to make sure Mr. Calhoun wasn't looking. Allison grabbed Max's hand and Sunny followed closely as they dashed down the hall and around a corner. A minute later, Raj came running up, panting. "We did it! Calhoun didn't see anything," he said.

"Oh no!" said Max. He was looking down at Sunny, who was becoming more **agitated**, stepping back and forth in front of Max, watching his face, and yelping.

"Come on," said Allison. "Ms. Sante's office is down here." Allison ran and the others followed. When they arrived at her office door, Allison tried to turn the handle. "It's locked!" she shouted over the sound of the alarm.

When she turned around, she saw Max lower himself to the floor, then slowly lie down. "Please don't leave," he said. As Allison and Raj knelt down beside Max, Sunny put both paws on his chest. Max reached his arm around the golden dog.

Then Max's eyes closed halfway and his arms began to shake. Sunny stayed where he was, looking **placidly** at Max.

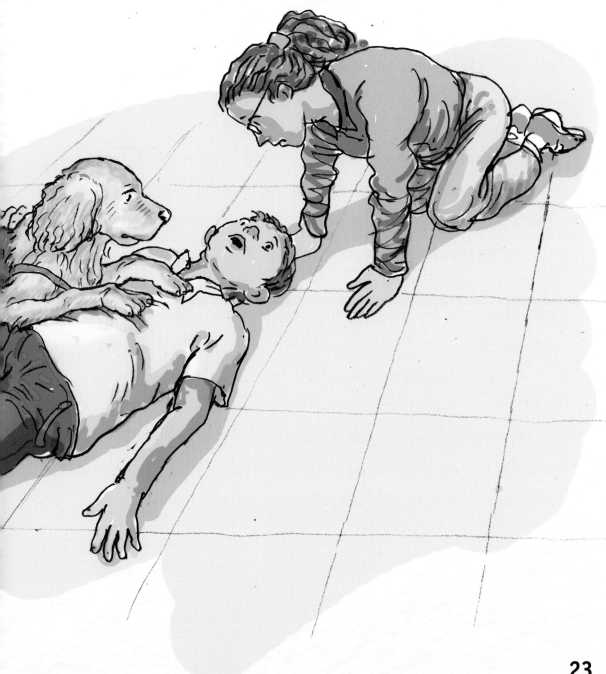

"What do we do?" asked Raj as he stared at Max, whose left leg began to twitch. "Should we go for help?"

"We can't leave him!" said Allison. Just then, the clanging fire alarm finally stopped.

Suddenly, Allison and Raj heard a voice coming from down the corridor. "Max? Are you there?"

"We're over here!" yelled Allison. "Quick!"

Allison and Raj saw Ms. Sante running down the hall. When she arrived, the nurse knelt down next to Max, gently took his wrist, and watched him. "When did the seizure start?" Ms. Sante asked.

"A few minutes ago," said Allison.

Max's body then began to calm. The twitching and shaking **subsided**, and he slowly opened his eyes. He looked at everyone around him.

Ms. Sante helped Max sit up, and she asked, "How are you feeling, kiddo?"

At first Max seemed confused. Then, after taking several deep breaths, he said, "I'm all right. Thanks to Sunny." He reached over and hugged his friend, whose tail was wagging happily.

CHAPTER 5

Luckier Than a King

In early November, the day for the class presentations finally arrived. The class partners presented many interesting topics about ancient Egypt, including the importance of the Nile River and the meaning of the famous pyramids. Raj made everyone laugh by describing how some Egyptians made their dead pets into mummies, adding that they probably liked them more than their human friends.

Allison and Max's presentation was the last one. Sunny sat quietly between them in front of the class as the partners described the discovery of King Tut's tomb nearly 100 years ago. They discussed how the **pharaohs** were treated as gods. Allison talked about how King Tut was called "the Boy King" since he died so young, and Max finished the presentation.

"One **theory**," said Max, "is that he had a disease that ran in his family. Some scientists now think that King Tut had epilepsy, and that falling down a lot led to his early death."

The classroom was very quiet. Some students looked nervously at each other. Tony's mouth hung wide open.

"But I guess King Tut just wasn't born at the right time," Max continued. "Today we have medicine for epilepsy and awesome

helpers like Sunny." The dog lifted his head toward Max and gave a soft bark. "I'm the lucky one. Luckier than a king."

The class burst into applause, and Sunny gave another quick, happy bark. He seemed to be smiling.

Mr. Calhoun tried to speak loud enough to be heard over the noisy students. "All right, the bell has rung. Time to head out." The students gathered their coats and backpacks, each one petting Sunny on their way out.

It was a week after the presentations, and today had been the first Sunny Share Day. It was Max's idea. He had wanted to set up a time when everyone could pet Sunny. Ms. Sante agreed to come into class once a week, so she would be there to watch Max while Sunny enjoyed some time off.

Max, Allison, and Raj were the last to leave the classroom. As the three walked home together, Allison handed some of the Golden Sunrise crackers she had packed to Raj and Max.

"I can't believe Mr. Calhoun is already talking about another research project," said Allison. She ate one cracker, and then fed one to Sunny, who gladly gulped it down.

"I know," said Raj. "It's like he wants us to keep learning or something."

Allison turned and made a face at him.

"The projects don't bother me," said Max. He also fed a cracker to Sunny. "I sort of like them . . . but maybe next time I'll get a *good* partner." He smiled broadly at Allison.

"Ha-ha," she said, and nudged him in the shoulder. Just then, the group arrived at Mrs. Baxter's house. Gizmo ran up to them and started to bark wildly at Sunny. Sunny ignored the noise, sat down next to Max, and waited patiently for another Golden Sunrise.

Sunny on Alert!
A Seizure-Alert Dog Story

1. How do you think Max feels when he first comes into the class?

2. What is happening in this scene?

3. How did Sunny help Max during his seizure? Be sure to include specific examples.

4. Describe the relationship between Allison and Max. How does it change over the course of the story?

5. Why does Max say he's "Luckier than a king"? Do you agree? Give your reasons.

agitated (AJ-ih-*tay*-tid) becoming nervous or worried

ancient (AYN-shuhnt) belonging to a time long ago

autism (AW-tiz-uhm) a condition that causes people to have trouble communicating with and relating to others

contagious (kuhn-TAY-juhss) able to be passed from one person to another

detect (dih-TEKT) to discover or notice something

diabetes (*dye*-uh-BEE-teez) a disease in which a person has too much sugar in his or her blood; it can cause a person to pass out

distracts (diss-TRAKTS) draws attention away

epilepsy (EP-uh-*lep*-see) a medical condition of the brain that causes seizures

intently (in-TENT-lee) seriously and with focus

pharaohs (FAIR-ohz) ancient Egyptian kings

placidly (PLASS-id-lee) calmly or peacefully

seizures (SEE-zhurz) sudden attacks that can cause a person to shake and even lose consciousness

service dogs (SUR-viss DAWGZ) dogs trained to do tasks for people with disabilities or health problems

subsided (suhb-SYD-id) became less intense

theory (THIHR-ee) an idea or belief based on limited information

tomb (TOOM) a place where a dead body is buried

unconscious (uhn-KAHN-shuhss) not awake; unable to think, hear, feel, or see

About the Author

Spencer Brinker lives and works in New York City. A designer by profession, he's enjoyed his recent foray into writing, and stories about animals are especially satisfying. While Spencer doesn't own a dog, he enjoys being in a city where hundreds of thousands of canines walk on the sidewalks and play in the parks. At home, his twin daughters have two lovable guinea pigs, Skittles and Strawberry, who add a playful element to his family life.

About the Illustrator

Robin Lawrie, a Scotsman who grew up in Vancouver, Canada, started his career as an author and illustrator in London. He now lives in an old barn in England, which has a bat sanctuary in the attic. He has illustrated almost 300 children's books, and he has written 21, mostly about one of his hobbies—downhill mountain biking. He has also adapted *The Lion, the Witch and the Wardrobe* and *The Magician's Nephew* into graphic novels.